GW01044224

For Danny and Matt – always proud of you.

Paw Kingdom
First edition published in 2021 in the United Kingdom

978-1-8383910-2-7

www.pawkingdom.co.uk

THE ENGLISH BULLDOGS ARE THE CHAMPIONS OF THE WORLD

Written and Illustrated by
Spencer Miller

Written by
Harrison Florio

WORLD CHAMPIONSHIP
THE KINGDOM TIMES
PUP CHAMPIONSHIP COMES TO ENGLAND!
1966
ENGLAND

Summer time had arrived in England,
Along with football 's biggest glory,
Every nation in the World tuning in,
Hoping for their fairytale story.

The biggest cup in world football,
Everyone filled with hope and cheer,
England's Bulldogs dreamed of victory,
Could this finally be their year?

Bulldogs 1 Fila Brasileiros 3
GO BULLDOGS!
DOG

The Bulldogs had never tasted success,
Having always come up short,
But this time they were back in England,
They had their home support.

Brazil had broken their hearts before,
Winning by three goals to one,
But after four years of hard–work,
They were ready for another cup run.

The most televised event of all time,
Broadcast all over the world,
France, Mexico and Uruguay awaited,
The Bulldogs ready for whatever unfurled.

They would cruise through their group,
Without conceding a single goal,
The fans celebrated every match,
Playing their crucial role.

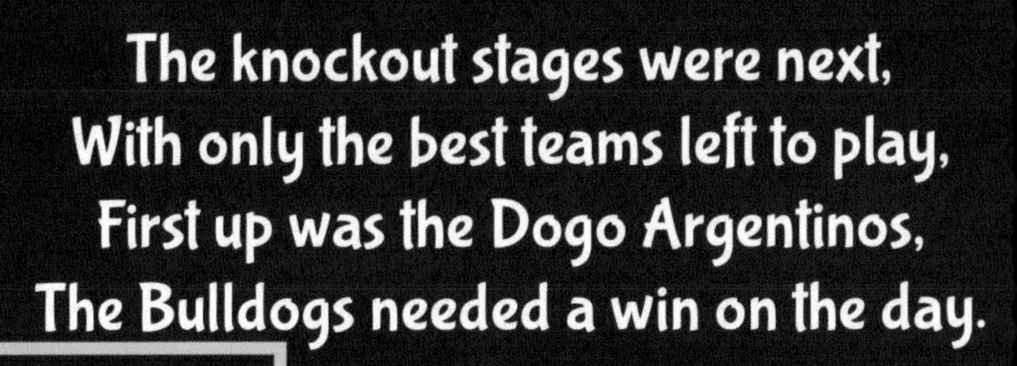

The knockout stages were next,
With only the best teams left to play,
First up was the Dogo Argentinos,
The Bulldogs needed a win on the day.

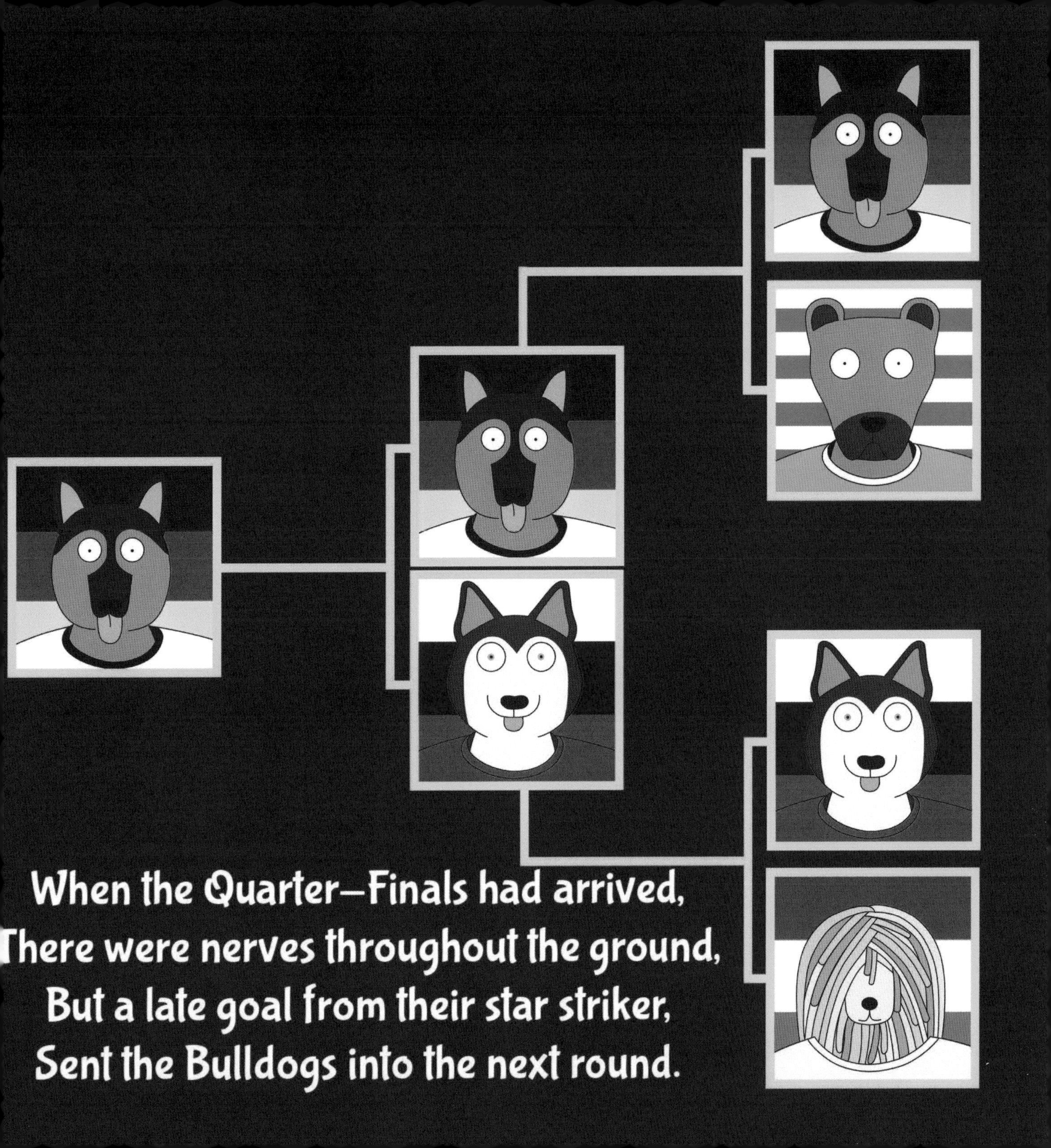

When the Quarter—Finals had arrived,
There were nerves throughout the ground,
But a late goal from their star striker,
Sent the Bulldogs into the next round.

GO BULLD
1
10
2

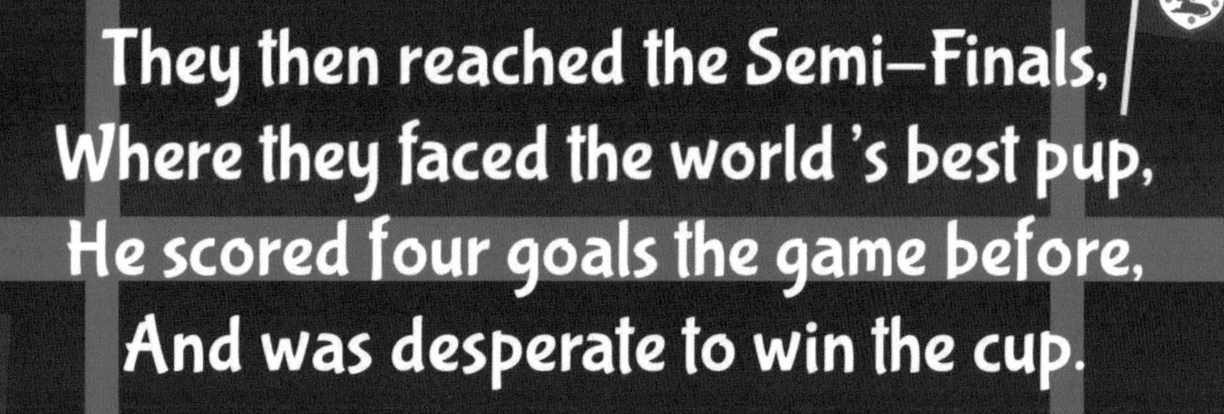

They then reached the Semi–Finals,
Where they faced the world 's best pup,
He scored four goals the game before,
And was desperate to win the cup.

But the Bulldogs stood firm,
Scoring twice against their rivals,
Despite the strikers best efforts,
The Bulldogs headed to the finals.

lldogs 0 Shepherds C
O BULLDOGS!
BU DOGS
1966
Shephe
30.7.66

Now the time had come,
To face their toughest test,
Having made it to the final,
They would have to face the best.

The German Shepherds stood in their way,
The Golden Bone was gleaming,
But with three pups on their shirts,
The Bulldogs never stopped dreaming...

GO SHEPHERDS!

But disaster struck early,
Just twelve minutes on the clock,
The Shepherds scored an early goal,
The Bulldogs were in shock!

The Bulldogs defence was shaky,
A mistake from the Centre–Back,
Meant they conceded a goal,
On the very first attack!

GO BULLDOGS!
GO SHEPHERDS!

The Bulldogs barked and growled,
Fighting hard to get back in the game,
The Shepherds had scored an early goal,
They needed to do the same.

Then the ball was crossed in with power,
The striker leaped up high,
And with his powerful snout,
Gave the Bulldogs their reply.

The tie was all level,
And the Bulldogs were on top,
But the Shepherds keeper was solid,
Catching and parrying without a drop.

Save after save from the goalie,
The Bulldogs couldn 't get through,
Despite all of their best efforts,
They couldn 't find goal number two.

GO BULLDOGS!

Bulldogs 2 Shepherds 1

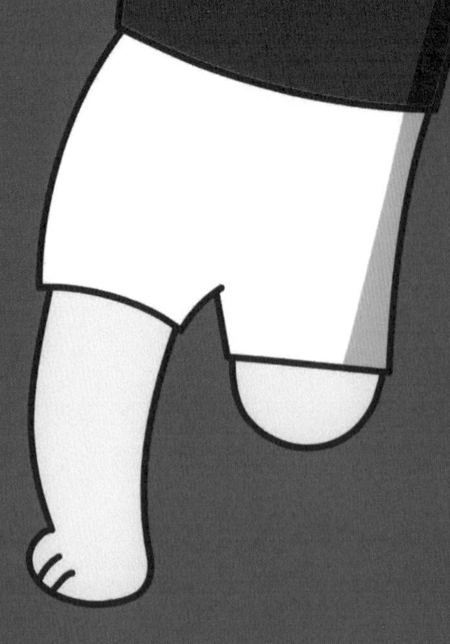

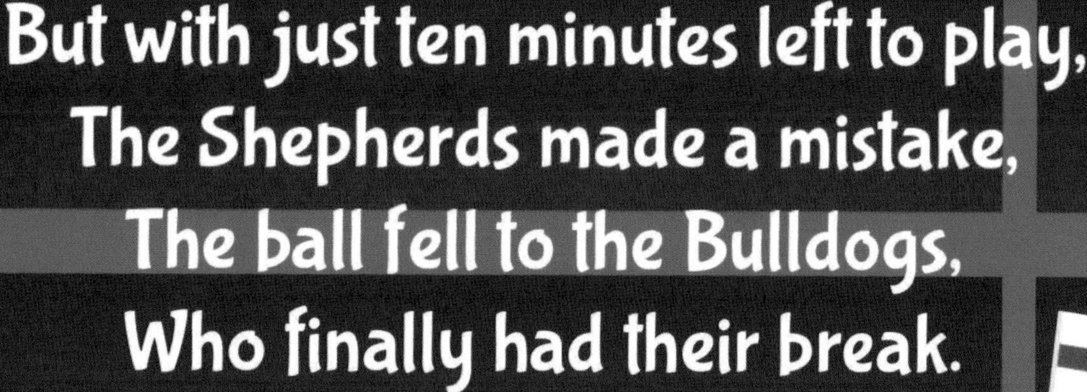

But with just ten minutes left to play,
The Shepherds made a mistake,
The ball fell to the Bulldogs,
Who finally had their break.

The ball was volleyed in,
The Bulldogs were in the lead,
Just ten minutes to hold on,
But nothing was guaranteed.

Just one minute left in the game,
The Shepherds got a shot away,
It bounced straight off the goalie,
The striker pounced on the ricochet!
GO SHEPHERDS!
GO BULLDOGS!

He slid the ball into the net,
To bring the game all square,
Equalising in the very last minute,
It was the Bulldogs worst nightmare!

Bulldogs 2 Shepherds 2
The final whistle then blew,
Just moments after the goal,
The Bulldogs were devastated,
The game had taken its toll.
GO SHEPHERDS!

Both teams were truly exhausted
Having given everything they had,
The match went into extra time,
The fans were going mad,

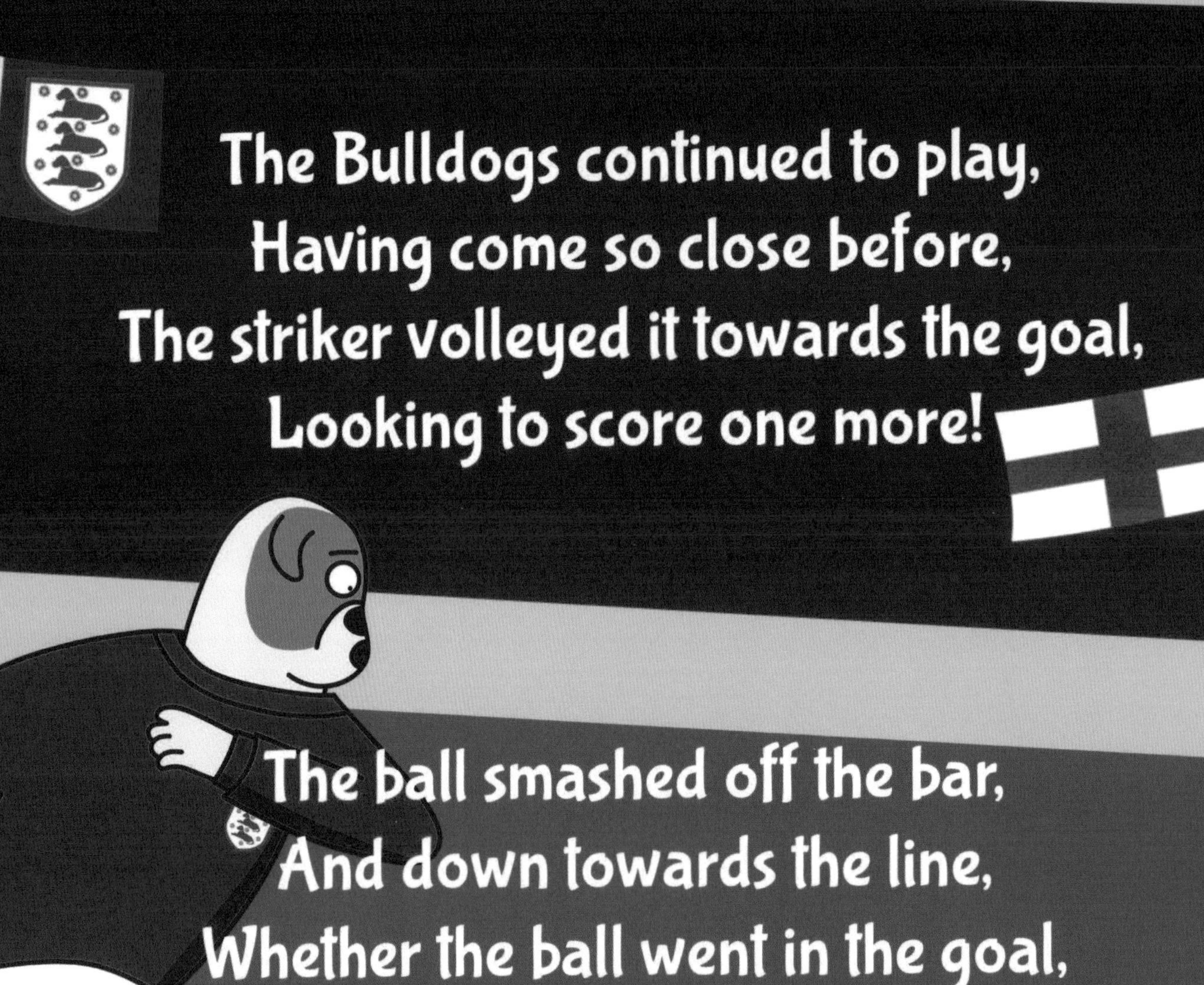

The Bulldogs continued to play,
Having come so close before,
The striker volleyed it towards the goal,
Looking to score one more!

The ball smashed off the bar,
And down towards the line,
Whether the ball went in the goal,
Is a question as old as time!

The German Shepherds were furious,
Crying "the ball didn't cross the line!"
But the referee awarded the goal,
And they were running out of time!

They had been behind before,
And had always found a way back,
Using all of their anger,
They mounted a last attack!

GO SHEPHERDS!

Bulldogs 3 Shepherds 2

This time there was no way through,
The Bulldogs stopped their advance,
Before one last counter-attack,
Which gave the striker a chance!

They thought it was all over,
And it really was now!
When the striker got his hat-trick,
And turned to take his bow.

GO BULLDOGS!
GO BULLDOGS!

So tell the story of the English Bulldogs,
Who finally brought football home!

BULLDOGS!

Printed in Great Britain
by Amazon

62569115R00020